Drusilla
the
Lucky Duck

by Errol Broome
illustrations by Sharon Thompson

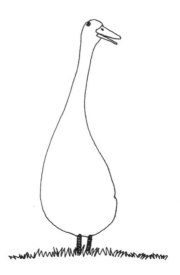

Annick Press Ltd.
Toronto • New York • Vancouver

First published in 1998 by Fremantle Arts Centre Press, Western Australia

Cataloging in Publication

Broome, Errol
    Drusilla the lucky duck / by Errol Broome ; illustrations by Sharon
Thompson. -- North American ed.

(Annick chapter books)
Originally published in Australia under title: Tough luck.
ISBN 1-55037-799-X (bound).--ISBN 1-55037-798-1 (pbk.)

    1. Ducks--Juvenile fiction. 2. Ducks as pets--Juvenile fiction.
I. Thompson, Sharon, 1958- II. Title. III. Series.

PZ7.B793D78 2003   j823   C2003-900054-0

The text was typeset in Century Schoolbook.

Distributed in Canada by: Published in the U.S.A. by:
Firefly Books Ltd.   Annick Press (U.S.) Ltd.
3680 Victoria Park Avenue   Distributed in the U.S.A. by:
Willowdale, ON   Firefly Books (U.S.) Inc.
M2H 3K1   P.O. Box 1338, Ellicott Station
                                   Buffalo, NY 14205

Printed and bound in Canada by Friesens, Altona, Manitoba

visit us at: **www.annickpress.com**

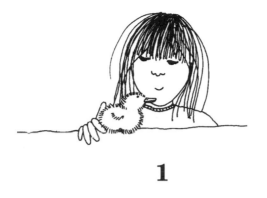

1

From the moment Carrie saw Drusilla, she had to have her.

She went to the breeders' market to buy a kitten, and came home with a duck.

Drusilla was just one day old, a warm puff of yellow, and light as air in Carrie's fingers. Something of a miracle, too, so tiny, yet so much bigger than the egg she'd come from only a day before. It was only her flat, rubbery bill that said, I'm a duck.

She was prettier than any picture Carrie had seen in books.

Mom had expected to go home with a kitten. "Are you sure?" she asked Carrie. "She won't be a cuddly little duckling for long. Will you love her when she's a big fat duck?"

"Of course," said Carrie, though she hadn't really thought about it.

The man wrapped Drusilla in tissue paper, as if she might break, and lifted her gently into a box. "Get home as quickly as you can, and keep her warm in a big box for three weeks."

Mom sighed. A kitten would have been easier.

"Make sure you read these instructions," said the man, "and the duck will be your friend for life."

Carrie read the booklet going home in

the car. "It says I can train my duck to come when she's called."

"What about the poo?" asked Mom.

"Uh-uh, sorry. No toilet training."

"Oh, dear, I didn't think to ask about that."

"But they eat all the slugs and snails in the garden."

"Wonderful!" said Mom. "I won't have to worry about my silver beet."

The Glovers' garden was small and neat, with everything in its place. Herbs grew around the kitchen door, and a few rows of vegetables up the back. Mom and Dad knew about gardens because it was their business. All week they looked after plants in their Garden Corner nursery, so they kept their own garden simple and easy-care.

They liked to sit on the back patio and

relax on Saturdays, and that's where Mom and Carrie found Dad when they came home from the market.

Dad leaned so far back on his chair that it tipped him onto the bricks. "Do I really hear what you're telling me? A duck!"

"They make good pets," said Carrie.

"One day it'll be a big, fat duck."

Mom nodded. "That's exactly what I said."

"It won't survive that long," said Mungo. "Don't worry."

Big brothers never said anything nice. Carrie screwed up her nose at him.

She'd show him. She'd show them all. They tried to put her off everything she wanted to do. Well, they were too late. She planned to have the duckling for a very long time.

"Mmm," mumbled Dad. "Another animal to come to a sad end." Like all the others. The goldfish had caught white spot disease and died slowly, one after the other. The canary had escaped and been gnawed by the neighbors' cat. Nobody knew what happened to the rabbit. One day it was healthy and the next it was dead in its cage.

"No," said Carrie. "Ducks can live as long as dogs, if you look after them."

"We'll see," said Dad in his wise voice. She wished he wouldn't talk like that.

"What happened to the cat idea?" asked Mungo.

"This was cuter."

9

Carrie knew straight away it was the wrong thing to say. Now Mungo was thirteen, he didn't like anything cute.

Dad waved her towards the house. "If you want it to survive, you'd better get it inside now. Mom'll find you a box and a light for heat, won't you, Jude?"

Mom pulled a face at him. "Go on reading the paper, then."

Carrie went on reading too. She lay on the floor beside the duckling's box and read until she knew the instruction booklet by heart.

"It says here that when a duckling hatches, it can attach itself to the first thing it sees. So if it sees a dog, it thinks the dog's the mother."

"Just as well you weren't there when this one hatched," said Mom.

"Lucky duck!" said Mungo. "Who'd want Carrie as a mother?"

"Shove off, Mungo."

"Yes, do," said Mom. She turned to Carrie. "You mean, they could think the box was their mother?"

"It doesn't have to be alive, but it must move," said Carrie.

"So it could be a wheelbarrow," said Mom. "Or a motorbike, even. Poor little ducks."

"My mother, the wheelbarrow!" said Mungo.

"Will you *listen*!" said Carrie. "Because it isn't too late. I can still train her if I start now."

2

Every day, Carrie lifted Drusilla from her box and lay on the floor beside her. Drusilla looked at Carrie, head cocked to one side, her tiny dark eyes like damp jewels, trusting her.

She called Drusilla's name and quacked to her. Slowly Carrie moved away, quacking softly.

Drusilla followed. When Carrie stopped, she snuggled against her legs. Carrie quacked and Drusilla answered in a tiny duck voice.

When Carrie sat down, Drusilla clambered over her legs and onto her lap. *Quark-uck-uck-uck.*

Steff came around to see the new duckling. She liked pretty things. You could tell that just by looking at her. Everything about her was bright and fresh as a new morning. She could wear her clothes—a white shirt even— all day without getting dirty. When Steff grew up, she was going to be a model.

Carrie couldn't make up her mind when people asked what she wanted to be. So she said she'd be a nurse and look after things.

Steff stroked the duckling and took photographs but didn't let Drusilla climb on her legs—just in case.

"They grow so quickly," she said.

Carrie knew that Steff would like Drusilla to be a duckling forever.

Soon, Drusilla was too big for the box and was ready to live outside the house. The yellow fluff firmed to longer, tighter feathers, and Carrie could see that Drusilla was changing to white.

Steff didn't think the duck was so pretty now.

"Not as pretty maybe, but nicer," said Carrie. "She knows her name, too."

Dad spent a weekend erecting a safe run with a small shelter in a corner of the garden. Mungo didn't help, even though he was going to be a builder when he grew up.

"I couldn't get around to a pond," said Dad. "You'll have to give her a sprinkle with the hose."

Early each morning Carrie fed the

duck before she had her own breakfast. Drusilla came when she called, quacking and tooting to greet her. Carrie smoothed and stroked the duck's feathers, then let her loose to find worms and slugs and snails in the yard. Drusilla dabbled and dipped among the flowers, and followed Carrie to the back door.

As Drusilla grew, her voice changed too. She was now a handsome white duck who called out *quart-onk-onk-onk*. Steff said it all sounded the same to her, but Carrie understood the language.

The morning Carrie slept in, Drusilla woke the whole house bellowing for food. *Quark quark-onk hoot holler*. Carrie knew what the duck was saying then too, and she didn't sleep in again.

Each afternoon, when Carrie came home from school, Drusilla was waiting at the back door. If Carrie didn't come to say hello, Drusilla knocked on the door with her bill. *Rap rap quark-onk-onk-onk. Hurry-up-up-up*. Carrie gave her a crust of bread and told her she was glad to be home.

Drusilla liked outings, too. Sometimes when Mom said yes, they took her out in the car. When it rained so hard that sensible people stayed inside, Carrie persuaded Mom to drive them to the park. She didn't want her duck to forget how to swim.

"It says NO DOGS," said Mom.

"But it doesn't say NO DUCKS."

Drusilla waddled across the lawn to the lake. Mom said she might get lost among the other ducks and Carrie would never find her again. But Carrie stood in the rain with water dripping off her coat, and as soon as she called, Drusilla streamed to the bank and nodded and chuttered after her.

Carrie wiped the duck's feet before lifting her into the car, but her feathers were dry to touch.

Other times they took the duck to Garden Corner. While Mom helped customers, Drusilla played in the fountain.

Derek, who worked there, leaned on his rake and beamed.

"Gosh, never thought I'd see better than a clay duck around here."

Drusilla showed off in the fountain, up-tailing and wing-flapping and flicking water from her feathers.

Mrs. Dibbs, who lived opposite, walked her toddlers across whenever she heard that the duck had arrived. Chloe and Josh brought bread and big grins and slopped to their elbows around the edge of the fountain.

Mrs. Dibbs agreed with Derek. She'd never have a clay duck in her garden now she'd seen the real thing.

"It's nearly human, that duck," said Derek. His long, lean body in overalls reminded Carrie of a runner bean, except that Derek was old and nice— and she hated runner beans.

"She doesn't have a pond at home,"

explained Carrie as the duck went about her act.

"Bring her here any time," said Derek. "I like having her around."

3

Not everyone liked Drusilla.

One Saturday morning, Dazz called on Mungo without knocking.

The moment he stepped into the yard, Drusilla began squawking. She dashed across the grass, neck stretched, beak wide, intent on driving him away.

"Yikes!" yelled Dazz, and turned to run.

Drusilla raced after him, snapping at his heels. She fastened her beak around his ankle.

Dazz leaped into the air and kept jumping, trying to shake the duck off. "Help!"

Carrie watched through the window. She waited until Drusilla let go, then she turned to Mungo, as slowly as she could. "You'd better let Dazz in the front door. I think he's scared of ducks."

Dazz's face was red when he came into the kitchen. "What's wrong with that duck!"

"You," said Carrie. Drusilla was better than any watchdog.

"I nearly swallowed my bubble gum!"

Pity you didn't, thought Carrie. The wad was so big it pushed out the side of his cheek. "I thought you had mumps."

Mom came into the kitchen and peered at the floor. "Who didn't wipe their feet?"

Mungo stared at the slimy smudges on the vinyl. "That blasted duck! Squelchy Poo, that's what you should call it."

Carrie pretended she hadn't heard.

"Just remember to wipe your feet," said Mom.

Mungo opened the door to the backyard. Dazz took a step, then stopped.

"It's OK," said Mungo. "It knows you now. Stupid duck, we're lucky if we can find a clean spot to sit outside these days."

He and Dazz sat on the bricks playing loud music, so Carrie couldn't hear what they were saying. And they couldn't hear what she was saying. "How dare he call Drusilla that name!" she said.

"Don't worry," said Mom. "She won't come when he calls."

When Dazz left for home, he threw his bubble gum away. Carrie thought he looked a lot better, but she didn't tell him.

In the yard, Drusilla gabbled among pots on the patio. She tossed her head and coughed.

Carrie leaned closer to the window. "Something's wrong! Look at Drusilla!"

The duck shook her head from side to side. *Quark gargle gulp*.

Carrie ran into the yard. She steadied Drusilla in her arms. "Quick, Mom! There's something in her throat."

"Is it stuck?"

"I can't see."

Drusilla was like a child at the doctor's. She didn't want to be helped. She flapped and fought and cried.

"Hold her neck," said Mom. "But not

too tight. We don't want to strangle her."

"What is it, can you see?"

Mom forced the duck's bill open with her fingers. "It's ... I think ... it's bubble gum."

"I knew it," said Carrie. "Don't let it go down. Can you get it?"

Drusilla flapped and chuttered. *Quark-oik-oik-oik.*

"Where's Mungo?" cried Carrie. "He could at least help us."

"Never mind Mungo," said Mom. "Hold her upside down."

"How do I do that?" Carrie struggled to hang Drusilla by a leg and a wing.

"She's heavy ... I haven't done this before."

Mom bent till her head almost touched the ground. She could see the ball of gum in the duck's throat. "I'll get it ... I can get it ... nearly ... it's a bit stuck ... it's hard ... but it's coming ... here ... now ... see!"

She dragged the gum from Drusilla's bill and held it high. "What a plug! It's a wonder the poor duck didn't choke to death."

"How could Dazz throw it away like that?" said Carrie. "Boys make me *so* mad." Who'd have a brother?

"Drusilla will be OK now," said Mom. "She's a pretty tough duck."

Carrie led her duck back to the run and sat there until Drusilla waddled into the shelter to rest. When I grow up, thought Carrie, I'll be a doctor and know what to do when ducks swallow bubble gum.

As she turned back to the house, Mungo was watching from the kitchen window. He moved away when he saw her.

"The duck will be all right," Mom said to Mungo. "Don't worry."

"Hmph!" he said, and pulled on his boots. "I'm going out."

He went quickly, without saying where he was going. And without saying sorry.

4

Dad hated working on Saturdays. When he came home, he flung his cap on the hall stand and yelled, "Where is everyone?"

He found Mom and Carrie in the kitchen, and flopped on a chair beside them. "Some people have a good life," he grumbled.

"You didn't ask what we've been doing," said Mom.

"Sorry, Jude. You know, all afternoon

I've been thinking it's time we had a holiday."

"Good!" said Carrie. "Where are we going?" They hadn't been anywhere for years.

"I haven't made up my mind yet."

"Half the fun's talking about it," said Mom.

Yes, thought Carrie. Then she remembered Drusilla. You couldn't put a duck in a quackery, like a cattery or a kennel. She went suddenly quiet and hoped Dad would forget about holidays.

"What would you say to the mountains?" he asked.

"Great idea," said Mom. "I'd love it."

Carrie thought about it. "That might be all right." If they took a little house in the mountains, Drusilla could go too. She'd like it there.

"I'll see what I can do," said Dad. "By the way, where's Mungo?"

"Gone out," said Carrie.

"I can see that."

"He didn't say where—he just went."

"It's only that I've remembered," said Dad, "he has a school camp in the July holidays, hasn't he?"

"That's all right," said Mom. "He'll have his holiday and we can have ours."

Carrie couldn't believe what Mom said. "You mean ... go without him?"

"I suppose we'll have to," said Dad.

A holiday in the mountains without Mungo! Things were getting better and better.

Mungo came home and dropped a book on the table. He spoke to Carrie without looking at her. "I saw this on a table outside the shop. You can have it if you like."

Carrie picked it up. *Ducks—and How to Rear Them*. "Mungo! Did you buy this for me?"

He shrugged. "Chuck it out if it's no good."

"Thanks." She knew why he'd bought it. "Thanks a lot."

"It's nothing."

It wasn't nothing to Carrie. She sat down to read. The book had everything she needed to know, with sections on feeding and health and laying and breeding.

30

"Don't you want any dinner?" asked Mom.

"I *am* hungry."

An hour had passed while she read about feathers and bills and the duck's boat-shaped body that suited it for life on a pond.

"And it says here that a diet of barley and milk fattens birds for the table. What does that mean?" She turned the page and read aloud. "'Young ducklings will roast or fry perfectly, but older birds are better cooked in a casserole.'"

Cooked! What is this? She read on.

Orange Duck

    one 2 kg duckling
    one orange, rind and juice
    one onion, chopped
    butter
    salt and pepper

She slammed the book shut. "You hateful pig!" she screamed at Mungo.

He held a bread roll in front of his mouth and stared at her. A shred of lettuce dropped to the table.

"I know why you bought that book!" She flung it against the wall.

"Hey, Carrie, go easy," said Mom.

"Mungo thinks it's funny, cooking ducks!"

Mungo lifted the piece of lettuce and held it between his fingers. "I never! I never looked at the book. It's true!" He swallowed hard, then glared at her. "Anyway, what would I care!"

Mom picked the book off the floor and smoothed the pages with her fingers. "It's a proper farming book, Carrie. That's why people breed ducks."

"Then why do they tell you how to look after them, if they're only going to eat them? And—I'm not hungry now!" She stormed out of the room and into the yard.

"I never knew," said Mungo grimly.

"It was a nice thing you did, Mungo," said Mom.

He watched Carrie go. "You can't do a thing that's right around here, since she got that stupid duck."

Carrie went out to talk to Drusilla. The duck scrambled to the gate to meet her. *Quark-onk-onk-onk*. Nobody else

gave her such a welcome. Drusilla was
her best friend, and was always pleased
to see her—not just at dinnertime.

She sat on a low stool and put Drusilla
on her lap. The duck plumped out her
feathers and coughed sleepily.

"Don't be afraid," mumbled Carrie.
"I won't let anything happen to you."

5

Dad came home waving his cap, and lobbed it gently on Carrie's head. "All fixed! We're off to the mountains in July."

"Good," said Carrie.

"I've booked an apartment for ten days."

"An apartment! Then what can I do with Drusilla?"

Dad heaved one of his thundering sighs. "Do we have to worry about a duck now!"

"We'll find someone," said Mom. "The neighbors will come in and look after her. We'll ask the Smiths."

"You can't ask the Smiths," said Dad. "They're far too old."

Carrie agreed. "The Smiths next door couldn't clean out the shed and change the water. What about the Russells?"

"You can't ask the Russells," said Mom. "They'd forget."

The Russells over the road couldn't even remember to put out their garbage on the right day.

"It's no good," said Carrie. "We can't leave Drusilla on her own. She'd think I was never coming back."

"Be sensible, Carrie!" said Dad. "I'm not letting a duck ruin our holiday."

"Then I'm not coming!"

Mom drew in her mouth like a closed

pouch. "As you wish," she breathed.

Carrie knew she was being selfish, making things difficult. But she wasn't thinking of herself. Drusilla was more important than any holiday.

"I won't go!" she said. Yet even as she spoke, she knew she'd have to go. When you were ten, you always gave in. What else could you do?

Mom didn't want to talk about it any more. It was still four weeks away, and you couldn't go on shouting at each other for four weeks. Maybe something would turn up. So, in the meantime, everybody pretended nothing was going to happen in July.

Carrie noticed that Mom was being extra-nice, though. Whenever she was free, she said, "Where would you like to go today?"

"Anywhere. I don't care."

"If you don't care, then we'll go to Garden Corner. I can work and Drusilla can have a swim."

Carrie was bundling Drusilla into the car when Steff arrived. "Can I come where you're going?"

"It's only to Garden Corner."

"That's OK."

"Get in, then."

Steff sat by the window furthest from the duck. She only pretended to like Drusilla. Carrie knew she was scared of getting dirty.

While Drusilla dabbled in the fountain, Steff wandered up and down the narrow paths, choosing the flowers she'd have in her garden one day. She was going to be a model with a bright, clean house and a garden full of camellias.

Derek picked a bloom from a camellia and gave it to her. "This is my favorite—'Debutante.'" He stood with his hand in the bib of his overalls and watched the duck. "Pretty thing, eh?"

Steff nodded. Drusilla was pretty, but she was messy too.

"Nice surprise, to see you today." He bent towards Carrie. "Anything wrong?"

"Not exactly, not yet. But I might have to go on holidays."

"Lucky you!"

"Except I can't take Drusilla—and I can't leave her either."

Derek tugged at his overall straps and chewed his lip. "Well ... I don't know ... I can't see why we couldn't take her for a while. Gosh, Mae would love a duck around the place. Just what she needs for company. And we've got the run I rigged up when we had Blackie."

"Would you?"

"Can't see why not. The duck'd be safe with us."

In one moment Carrie felt all the tight knots inside her unravel and slip away. She smiled at Derek. Everything would be all right now. She could trust Derek with her duck.

40

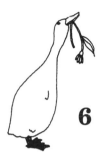

6

First, they had to get Mungo off to camp.

"Sleeping bag, groundsheet, towel, flashlight ..." Mom ticked things off on her fingers. "Don't forget some clothes to leave at Dazz's, for when you get back."

The camp would end before they returned from the mountains, so Mungo had arranged to spend the last three days at Dazz's house.

Mungo wasn't listening. He was too busy shaking his Walkman and holding it up to his ear. "Today, of all days!" He flung it on the bed. "The blasted thing's had it!"

Nobody cared much. "It'll do you good to listen to the bush for a change, instead of that awful music," said Mom.

Carrie only made things worse. "Bet you haven't packed your toothbrush," she said as he struggled out the door with his kit.

He poked a face at her and trudged towards the gate.

Carrie went to her bedroom, then caught up with him on the street. "Here," she called, "take my Walkman."

He turned around. "Eh?"

"Go on, take it. You'll miss the soccer if you don't have one."

His eyes said, What's come over her? but his voice said, "Gee, thanks."

"See ya!" she said, and ran back to the house.

"See ya!"

Packing up Drusilla came next. Carrie piled everything into a big box—water bowl with wire cover, food pellets, a sack of wood shavings, a big cabbage, and a list of instructions that began: *7 a.m.— feed and change water.*

Derek and Mae were waiting when the Glovers drove up to their door. Derek took the box and unpacked it in the old dog run. Mae fussed over the duck. She was as short as Derek was tall, with glasses that gave her eyes an owl-like look.

Wise old Mae, thought Carrie. She'll look

after Drusilla as if she were her own.

To Drusilla, it was just another outing. She didn't know she was there for ten days. Carrie tried to tell her, but Drusilla gabbled and chattered and poked in the grass for worms.

I'll miss her more than she'll miss me, thought Carrie when she said goodbye.

Mom said that once you got away, you stopped worrying about things at home, and it was nearly true. The mountain air didn't only take your breath away, it blew away your troubles.

The holiday apartments clung to the side of the mountain almost at the summit. Below, the ranges spread like a giant quilt, fold upon fold of misty mauves and mottled multi-greens.

Walking tracks snaked around the village, each turn opening up a fresh vista. Creeks gurgled in the hollows. Mountain people squinted at the sky and said the clouds were carrying snow.

Carrie waited for them to dump a white shawl across the village. She couldn't wait to see snow, even though Dad said it made your nose sting and your toes burn right through your boots. Each day, the clouds hung lower and heavier, bundling together to hold their load.

Sometimes Carrie remembered Drusilla and was glad her duck was in safe hands. She made friends with other children in the village. They walked and climbed and played volleyball on the uneven grass. Her cheeks tingled, warm in the cold air, and she was always hungry. In the evenings they roasted chestnuts and marshmallows around the fire.

The snow didn't fall until the last morning. As they drove away, Carrie looked back through the window at the spotty white curtain shrouding the village. She didn't want to leave on a day like this, but she was heading home.

And before home, Drusilla.

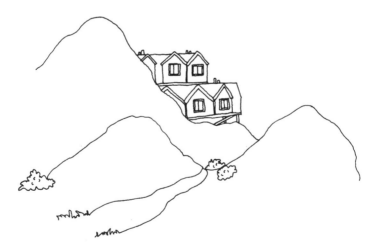

7

Dad sang most of the way to Derek and Mae's house. Inside herself, Carrie was singing too. It was only minutes now before she would see Drusilla again.

Mae came to the door. Everything about the house was quiet. "Did you have a good holiday?" she asked. "Derek's at work."

"How's Drusilla?" asked Carrie.

Mae's wise-owl eyes narrowed. "She's fine, I'm sure."

"Don't you *know*?"

"She isn't here now—we couldn't keep her. The neighbors complained."

"Complained?" said Carrie. No one had ever complained before. "What happened?"

"The noise! It was like nothing you've heard before!"

"But where is she? My duck!"

"Every morning, she woke us up—and the whole street."

"She was telling you ..." Carrie spoke through her teeth. "... she was hungry."

"I've never been an early riser, it's not my habit." Mae

didn't want to stop talking now. "Bit of a night owl, I am. And then, at the crack of dawn each morning, this rumpus! On and on and on, enough to wake the dead."

"But *please* ... where is she?"

Mae held the door open. "Come in. We didn't want to worry you ... spoil your holiday ... so Derek fixed it up. He wrote it down ... yes ... here it is ... He arranged for your friend Steff to look after her."

"Steff!" said Carrie. "She doesn't even like ducks."

"She and her father came to pick her up. They seemed to know what to do."

All the mountain pink drained from Carrie's cheeks. Her mouth was dry and floury. She turned away. "Come on, Dad. Quick!"

Dad didn't sing in the car any more. "Who'd keep ducks!"

The drive to Steff's house seemed to take forever.

Steff saw the car and ran to the gate to meet them. "Did you have a good holiday?"

That's what Mae had asked. "Until today," said Carrie. "Have you got Drusilla?"

"We did, for a while, but ..." She screwed up her nose. "She made such a mess. Mom couldn't hack it."

Carrie didn't want to hear any more. *"Where is she?"*

Steff's mother came out of the house. "I'm so sorry. We tried, but we just couldn't keep her. The mess! We walked the droppings right through the house. I'll have to get all the carpets shampooed."

"But where *is* she?" Carrie tried not to scream.

"We thought about it, and we were nearly desperate, until Steff remembered those children who liked the duck so much. And I contacted their mother."

"You mean Chloe and Josh?"

"That's them. Their mother, Zoe Dibbs, said it might be fun to have a duck for a while. So, last Sunday they came and collected her."

"Back into the car," said Dad wearily.

8

"How could they do this to my duck?" mumbled Carrie.

Passing her on, like a bit of baggage. She couldn't be sure Drusilla was *anywhere* now.

Mom turned around and patted her knee. "Don't look so grim, Carrie. She'll be fine, you'll see."

Dad stopped the car outside the Dibbses' house. "Let's see what happens here."

Chloe and Josh scrambled to the door

and pressed their mouths against the glass. "Duck! Are you bringing back the duck?"

Carrie caught her breath. "Isn't she here?"

Zoe Dibbs came out, smiling. "Hello! We've had lots of fun while you've been away."

"But, what about Drusilla?"

"The duck's fine. Josh and Chloe loved having Drusilla. She looked after the children, too, really protected them."

"Ye-e-es," said Carrie, "but then ... what?"

"Then we had a problem. She chased Garth away when

he came to fix the drain. She wouldn't let him near the place, really went for him, hissing and barking and biting him around the ankles. He ran for his life."

"She didn't like him," said Carrie.

"But we had to get the drain fixed—and Drusilla grew to like him. He came back later with barley and milk. He knew what to feed her, all right."

"Did you say ... barley and milk?" There was something in the book about barley and milk. The words came back to her: *fattens birds for the table—older birds are better cooked in a casserole ...*

"Yes, barley and milk," said Zoe. "He came and fed her every day after that. Fattening her up, he said. Then he told us he'd take her off our hands."

"You mean ... he took Drusilla?"

Zoe nodded. "Yesterday. It suited me.

I had a man coming today to fix the light."

"Quick!" Carrie's heart began to thump against her chest. "Quickly, Dad!"

Dad sighed, as if the hunt would never end. "Where does Garth live?"

"It isn't far," said Zoe. "Here's the address."

"Faster, Dad, faster." Carrie knew what Garth had in mind.

"This is getting beyond a joke, running around the neighborhood looking for a duck," said Dad.

"Faster, Dad, faster."

Dad drove at the same pace. "I'm not risking our necks for any animal."

"It's just that ..." Carrie couldn't bring herself to say the words. "*Please* drive faster, Dad."

"If you want us to have an accident ..."

"It was *all* an accident." Carrie's dull voice was lost between the seats. "Going away was an accident."

She didn't know whether she'd see Drusilla again.

9

"Will we ever get home, do you think?" Mom asked. "Mungo will be waiting and no one will be there."

"Forget Mungo! What about my duck?"

"I'm getting there as fast as I can," said Dad. "This looks like the street. What number was it?"

"Number 37," said Carrie.

"That's it." Mom pointed a few houses ahead. "The one with the orange tree."

Orange duck! "Stop!" screamed Carrie.

"Calm down," said Dad. "We aren't quite there yet."

Carrie jumped from the car and banged on the front door before Mom and Dad had unfastened their seat belts. "Anyone home?" Nothing. "Nobody's here," she said. "What do we do now?" This was her last chance to find Drusilla.

Mom and Dad didn't look so worried. "Go on, try again."

Carrie banged on the door with both fists. The door rattled and shook, but nobody came.

"We can come back tomorrow," said Dad.

"Tomorrow!" How could he say that? "Don't you understand? Tomorrow will be too late."

"There isn't much else we can do," said Mom.

"Isn't there just! Well, I'm not waiting!" Carrie rushed down the front steps and around the side of the house towards the back.

A high wire fence blocked the way. She tried the gate, but it was locked.

"Let me in!" she shrieked, and shook the gate. It clattered and clanked, but still nobody came.

Dad put a firm hand on Carrie's shoulder. "Wait. Someone will come."

"I can't wait." She stopped and listened, and felt that the silence was trying to tell her something. "Things aren't right, I know it."

She began to climb the fence. The toes of her sneakers fitted into the spaces

59

between the wire. She hauled herself almost to the top.

"Come down!" said Mom. "You'll hurt yourself."

Carrie took no notice. She scrambled to the top and hoisted one leg and then the other over the bar. She slipped and slid down the other side, until she could jump to the ground.

"Come back!" Mom called, but Carrie kept going.

"Drusilla!" she called softly. She crept forward, hugging the side wall of the house, and found herself in the backyard. It was only small, with a patch of long grass, a clothesline, and a shed in the corner.

Carrie stood ankle deep in grass and looked about her. Drusilla had been here! She'd know a duck's droppings anywhere. "Drusilla!" she called again.

Then she noticed the back door was open. She tiptoed up the three wooden steps and peered through the screen into the kitchen. As she stared, a shadow flicked across the room and something bumped against the wall.

"Someone's there!" she cried. "Hello!"

There was no reply.

"I saw you! Let me in!"

Carrie heard Mom and Dad's cries outside the fence. She took no notice.

"Then I'm coming in!" she yelled.

As she opened the screen door, a man sidled from a hidden corner of the kitchen. "Oh, there *is* someone here," he said.

You knew I was here, Carrie said to herself. *You were hiding, I know it.*

She stood on the top step, holding the door open. "Where's my duck?"

"Duck?"

"I know you've got her."

He looked at Carrie, and over her head to the yard. "I'm afraid she ... she got away."

"Not again!"

"What d'you mean, not again?"

"I've been searching and searching. We've been everywhere."

He straightened his back and towered over Carrie. "Well, I'm sorry. I can't help you."

"Have you looked in your shed?"

"Of course I've looked in the shed." He pointed over his shoulder. "You can go now."

"I'm not going until I find Drusilla." She turned towards the shed, then stopped. "What's that?"

"It's people shouting at the fence. Do they belong to you?"

"I don't mean *them*." It sounded like a cough, and the shuffle of one thing brushing against another.

"I didn't hear anything else." He began to hum.

"Ssh! There it is again."

He hummed more loudly now.

"It's coming from the shed." She strode across the yard and yanked the door open. "Drusilla!" She was sure Drusilla was there.

The inside was dark and stuffy. When her eyes adjusted to the gloom, she saw a workbench, piled with paint cans and boxes of tools. Behind the bench, a rusty bicycle leaned against an old cupboard.

The muffled cough and shuffle was clear now, but there was no sign of Drusilla.

"Carrie, come back immediately!" she heard her father call.

"Nothing here!" said Garth, and moved to close the door.

What if he locks me in? thought Carrie. But he wouldn't, because Mom and Dad were outside the gate. She pushed past the mower and shifted the bicycle away from the cupboard.

Garth hummed loudly.

Carrie had her hand on the cupboard door. *What if Drusilla is already dead?* She stopped, her fingers around the knob. *But she's alive. I've heard her.* Though they were not the Drusilla sounds she knew. What had happened to her?

Carrie took a deep breath and turned the handle. All she saw was a burlap sack. But the sack moved! It scuffed against the cupboard walls, and a weak cluck came from inside.

She tore the sack open. "Drusilla!"

The duck struggled to stand. Her bill was fastened shut with an elastic band.

"What has he done to you?"

When she ripped off the band, Drusilla squawked in the rudest duck language Carrie had ever heard.

"What's going on?" Dad stood

beside her. His face was flushed and sweaty.

Mom stayed outside the shed, rubbing her knee. Carrie saw blood running down her shin. "You didn't have to climb the fence," she said.

"We've found the duck," Garth told them.

We've found the duck! "Yes, *I*'ve found her," she said. She laid her head against Drusilla. "Are you all right?"

Quark-onk-onk-onk.

"I'm taking you home," said Carrie.

"Look ..." said Garth. He turned to Carrie and Mom and Dad in turn. "I've grown to like the duck. How about you let me buy her? Fair's fair—I'll give you five dollars."

"Five dollars! For my duck! There's no way I'd let you have her." Carrie put

66

Drusilla down on the grass and stood up to face him. "I know what you were going to do. You hid her when you heard the doorbell."

"I ... er ... was getting her ready for ..."

Carrie put her hands over her ears. "Don't tell me!"

"... for the trip home. I was expecting you."

Carrie's face was red. "I don't believe you." She glared at him. "And if you want to know, this is a very tough duck."

"Tough?"

"Yes, *very* tough. And I don't take my duck anywhere in a sack." Drusilla stood beside her like a bodyguard. "We walk!" said Carrie.

She marched up the back steps, with Drusilla strutting at her heels. Behind them came Mom and Dad, through the kitchen, past the table with oranges and onions on it, along the passage, and out the front door.

"What a day!" said Dad as he opened the car doors. "I feel as if I've never had a holiday."

"After all that, we left the water bowl and other stuff behind," said Mom.

They didn't seem important to Carrie. "We'll find something else." She cuddled Drusilla under her arm. "You're safe now," she whispered. "Garth won't ever want you again."

Drusilla quacked and chuttered and nudged Carrie's elbow.

"When I grow up," she said, "I'm going to run a quackery, where everyone can bring their ducks when they go on holiday."

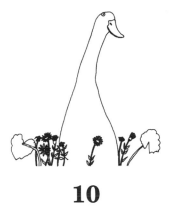

10

Mungo said he thought they were never coming home.

"So did we," said Dad. "We had some trouble finding the duck."

"I thought I'd never see her again," said Carrie. "And I was just in time."

"Phew!" said Mungo. "That's good, because I wouldn't have wanted to waste all my work."

"What work?" Carrie asked.

"Come and see."

They carried their bags into the house

and followed Mungo into the yard.

"While I was staying at Dazz's joint, there was nothing to do. Well, nothing much. So we came around here each day and we built a pond."

There it was, on one side of the patio, a sunken pond made of fiberglass, with a proper drain at the bottom.

Carrie set Drusilla down on the bricks. She waddled a few steps, looked around, and headed for the water.

"Gee, Mungo, thanks."

He stood, smiling, watching the duck glide and spin in small circles. Then he turned to Carrie and shrugged. "It's nothing."

Carrie punched him on the arm. Mungo always said everything was nothing, but some big brothers were really *something*.

About the author

Errol Broome grew up in Perth, where she studied Arts at the University of Western Australia and worked as a journalist at the *West Australian*. She now lives in Melbourne. An award-winning writer, her books include *Nightwatch* and *What a Goat!*